WHY WORMS?

Gillian Davies

Illustrated by Robin Kramer

GALLERY BOOKS
An Imprint of W. H. Smith Publishers Inc.
112 Madison Avenue
New York City 10016

Andrew had a drawing book—a big, fat, enormous drawing book. It had lots of "please-fill-me-up" pages, so Andrew drew on them with his fat red crayon.

He drew cars, cats, and cowboys. He drew kings, queens, and astronauts.
He drew horses, hills, and helicopters.

But most of all, he drew worms—lovely, wriggly worms!

"Why worms?" asked his mom.

"Because I like them," said Andrew, "and they're easy."

So Andrew drew worms—long, lean curling ones that wound all over the page.

He drew tiny, squished-up ones, in the corners.
He drew worms on their backs, on their fronts, and
upside-down.

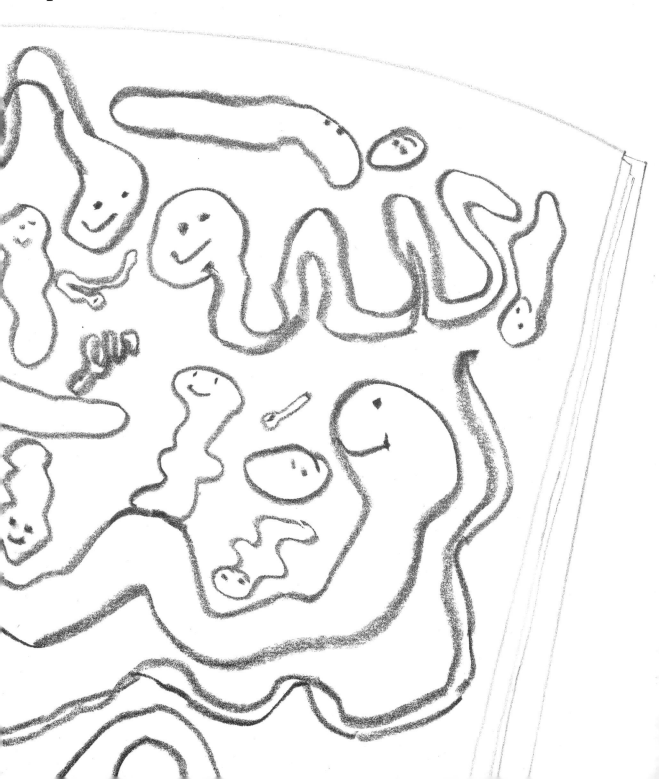

There were worms so thin they tangled up like string, and worms so fat they filled a whole page with one wriggle.

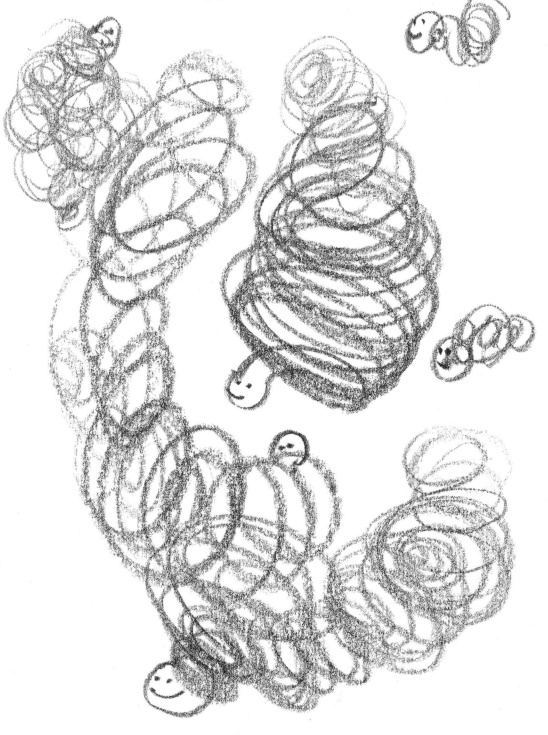

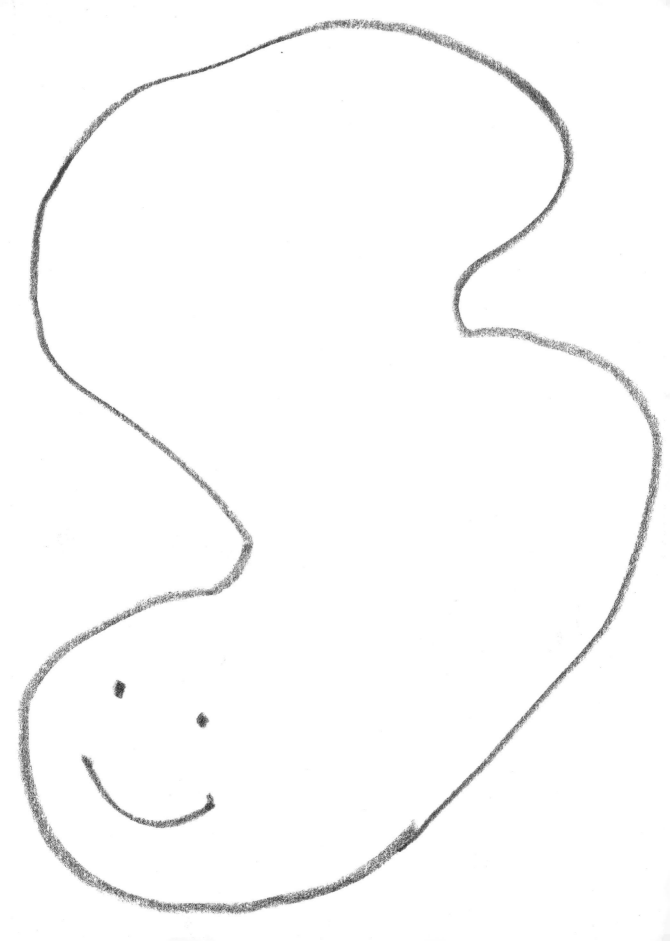

Andrew drew worms in cars, under cats, and in cowboy hats!
He drew worms that rode horses, crawled over hills, and waved out of helicopters.
He drew and drew until there were no worms left and the big, fat, enormous drawing book was full!

Andrew looked around for somewhere else to draw.
But there was only the wall—the beautiful, white
bedroom wall!

So he drew an especially big, happy worm. It weaved its way along by Andrew's bed and peeped around the corner to smile over his pillow.

"Come and see my happy worm!" shouted Andrew.
But his mom didn't like the worm at all. In fact, she was very angry.
She made him wash the worm away with a wet cloth.

So Andrew was sad and he drew sad worms on his pillowcases.

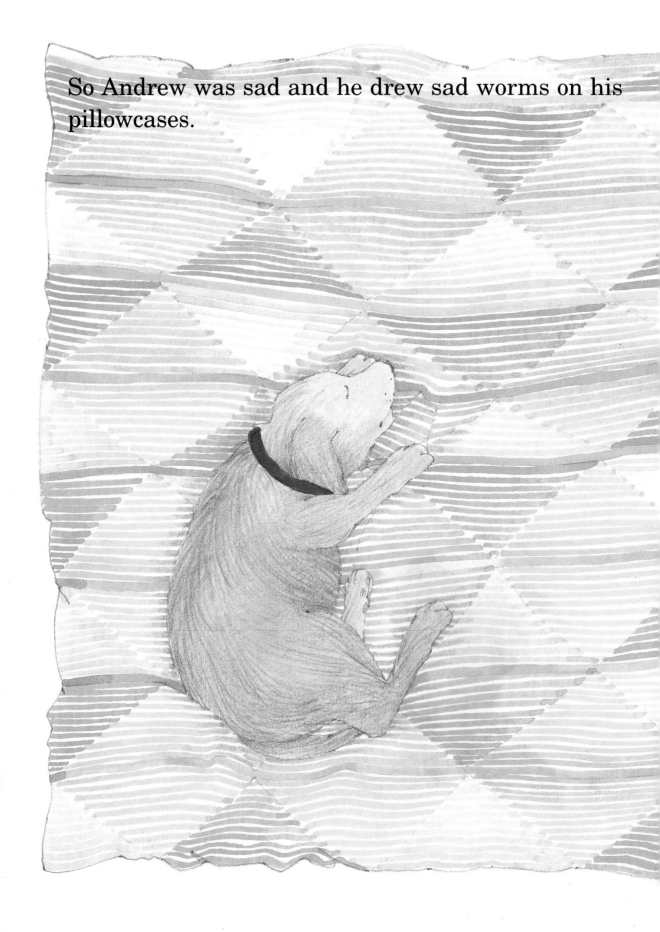

His mom didn't like the sad worms either. She took away his crayon—and his pillowcase to wash!

"Time for bed," she said. So Andrew had to dream of worms instead.

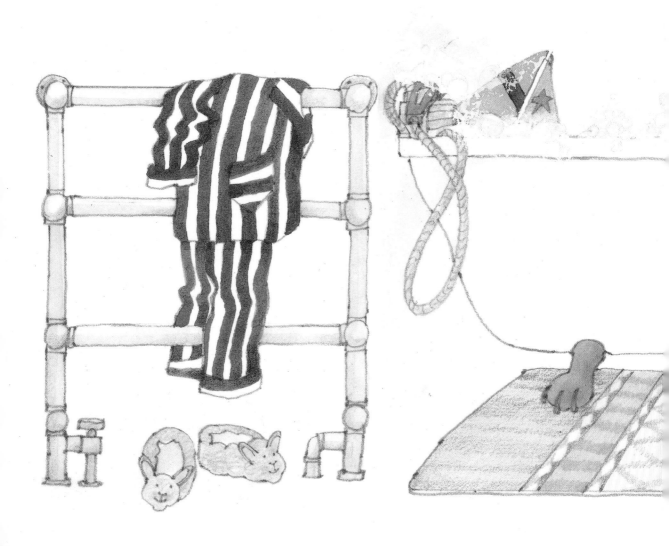

The next day Andrew wanted to draw again.
"We're going shopping first," said his mom.

And Andrew's mom bought him a new, big, fat enormous drawing book with even more pages and an especially blue, blue crayon.

But Andrew was fed up with worms now, so he drew…

spiders instead!

First published in the United Kingdom in 1989 by William Collins Sons and Co. Ltd. This edition first published in the United States in 1989 by Gallery Books, an imprint of W.H. Smith Publishers, Inc., 112 Madison Avenue, New York, New York 10016. Produced for Gallery Books by Joshua Morris Publishing, Inc. in association with William Collins Sons and Co. Ltd. Text copyright © 1989 Gillian Davies. Illustrations copyright © 1989 Robin Kramer. All rights reserved. ISBN 0-8317-4454-5 Printed in Hong Kong.